The Grinny Granny Donkey

For Fiona, Archer and the original Grinny Granny herself,
Janice Clark. You will forever make me smile.
And for all the grandparents who sing and read to their grandchildren.
– Craig Smith

To Archer, may you always be filled with endless love and giggles,
and may you never forget that you have a marvellously magical
Scottish Granny who has melted hearts all over the world.
– Katz Cowley

heath: a stretch of open, unfarmed land

Text copyright © 2020 by Craig Smith
Illustrations copyright © 2020 by Katz Cowley

Library of Congress Cataloging-in-Publication Data available

ISBN 978-1-338-69227-3

10 9 8 7 6 5 4 3   21 22 23 24

Printed in the U.S.A. 40
This edition first printing, November 2020

Illustrations created in watercolours and faerie tears.
The text was set in Drawzing.

Book design by Smartwork Creative Ltd, www.smartworkcreative.co.nz

The Grinny Granny Donkey

Words by Craig Smith
Illustrations by Katz Cowley

SCHOLASTIC INC.

NEW YORK TORONTO LONDON AUCKLAND
SYDNEY MEXICO CITY NEW DELHI HONG KONG

There was a sweet donkey
who lived on the heath.

She was so funny
with her false teeth . . .

Hee Haw!

But her teeth kept falling out!

She was a
clunky donkey.

There was a sweet donkey who lived on the heath.
She was so funny with her false teeth . . .

Hee Haw!

But her teeth kept falling out!

She loved to sip her favorite brew
and dunk her biscuits in it.

She was a
**dunky-drinky,
clunky donkey.**

There was a sweet donkey who lived on the heath.
She was so funny with her false teeth . . .

Hee Haw!

But her teeth kept falling out!

She loved to sip her favorite brew,
dunk her biscuits in it . . .

and fall asleep in the afternoon sun.

She was a **zonky**,
dunky-drinky,
clunky donkey.

There was a sweet donkey who lived on the heath.
She was so funny with her false teeth . . .

Hee Haw!

But her teeth kept falling out!

She loved to sip her favorite brew,
dunk her biscuits in it,
fall asleep in the afternoon sun . . .

then go for walks with her jewelry on.

She was a **clinky-clanky**, zonky, dunky-drinky, clunky donkey.

There was a sweet donkey who lived on the heath.
She was so funny with her false teeth . . .

Hee Haw!

But her teeth kept falling out!

She loved to sip her favorite brew,
dunk her biscuits in it,
fall asleep in the afternoon sun,
go for walks with her jewelry on . . .

and she always dressed smartly.

She was a **swanky**,
clinky-clanky, zonky,
dunky-drinky,
clunky donkey.

There was a sweet donkey who lived on the heath.
She was so funny with her false teeth . . .

Hee Haw!

But her teeth kept falling out!

She loved to sip her favorite brew,
dunk her biscuits in it,
fall asleep in the afternoon sun,
go for walks with her jewelry on,
dress smartly . . .

and she played her banjo to relax.

She was a
plunky-plinky,
swanky,
clinky-clanky,
zonky,
dunky-drinky,
clunky donkey.

There was a sweet donkey who lived on the heath.
She was so funny with her false teeth . . .

Hee Haw!

But her teeth kept falling out!

She loved to sip her favorite brew,
dunk her biscuits in it,
fall asleep in the afternoon sun,
go for walks with her jewelry on,
dress smartly and play her banjo to relax . . .

BUT if she hadn't had a visit from her family
in a while, she would sometimes get grumpy and cranky!

She was a **granky**,
plunky-plinky,
swanky,
clinky-clanky,
zonky,
dunky-drinky,
clunky donkey.

There was a sweet donkey who lived on the heath.
She was so funny with her false teeth . . .

Hee Haw)!

But her teeth kept falling out!

She loved to sip her favorite brew, dunk her biscuits in it,
fall asleep in the afternoon sun, go for walks with her
jewelry on, dress smartly, play her banjo to relax,
and sometimes she got grumpy and cranky . . .

BUT when her son, Wonky, turned up with her cute
granddaughter, Dinky, that granky granny donkey got
so many cuddles and kisses that she couldn't get the
smile off her face for weeks!

She was a **grinny granny**, plunky-plinky, swanky, clinky-clanky, zonky, dunky-drinky, clunky donkey.

There was a **GRINNY GRANNY**
donkey who lived on the heath.
She smiled so much you could
see her false teeth . . .

Hee Haw!